Meet the
Parents

For Trudy, Alan, Freya, and Tira
—P. B.

For Jane and Dave
—S. O.

SIMON & SCHUSTER BOOKS FOR YOUNG READERS

An imprint of Simon & Schuster Children's Publishing Division

1230 Avenue of the Americas, New York, New York 10020

Text copyright © 2014 by Peter Bently

Illustrations copyright © 2014 by Sara Ogilvie

Originally published in 2014 by Simon & Schuster UK Ltd.

First U.S. edition 2014

All rights reserved, including the right of reproduction in whole or in part in any form.

SIMON & SCHUSTER BOOKS FOR YOUNG READERS is a trademark of Simon & Schuster, Inc.

For information about special discounts for bulk purchases, please contact Simon & Schuster Special Sales at 1-866-506-1949 or business@simonandschuster.com.

The Simon & Schuster Speakers Bureau can bring authors to your live event. For more information or to book an event, contact

the Simon & Schuster Speakers Bureau at 1-866-248-3049 or visit our website at www.simonspeakers.com.

Book design by Tom Daly • The text for this book is set in Baskerville and Lectra.

The illustrations for this book are rendered in mixed media: pencil, pastel, ink, paint, monoprint, and digital • Manufactured in China

0715 SUK

2 4 6 8 10 9 7 5 3

Library of Congress Cataloging-in-Publication Data • Bently, Peter, 1960– • Meet the parents / Peter Bently ; illustrated by Sara Ogilvie. • pages cm • A Paula Wiseman Book. • First published in 2014 by Simon & Schuster UK.

Summary: Although it sometimes seems that parents are just there to boss their children around, they are also good for many other things, from mending toys, kneecaps, and clothing to telling bedtime stories.

ISBN 978-1-4814-1483-8 (hardcover) • ISBN 978-1-4814-1484-5 (eBook) • [1. Stories in rhyme. 2. Parent and child—Fiction.] I. Ogilvie, Sara, illustrator. II. Title. • PZ8.3.B4466Mee 2014 • [E]—dc23

2013034757

Meet the Parents

Peter Bently   Sara Ogilvie

A Paula Wiseman Book

Simon & Schuster Books for Young Readers

New York London Toronto Sydney New Delhi

Sometimes you think that your mom and your dad are there just to nag you and boss you like mad.

Do this and do that—it's a terrible bore.
But here are some *more* things your parents are for . . .

Parents are handy as mending machines
for teddies and train tracks and kneecaps and jeans.

Parents are great to build mountains of sand on,

and lovely big heaters for warming your hands on.

Parents are sofas for putting your feet up,

and Dumpsters for bits that you don't want to eat up.

Parents are tent poles for dens that are wonky.

Dad is a horse,

and Mom is a donkey.

Parents are targets for ketchup. And hoses.

And hunters for toys that you left in the roses.

Parents are towels for
wiping your grime on.

They're whirlers and twirlers

and tree trunks to climb on.

Parents are grandstands to make you grow tall.

They're jotters

and blotters . . .

but that isn't all.

Parents sort out all your messes and muddles.

Parents remember.

Parents give cuddles.

Parents tell stories and tuck you up tight,
as snug as a bug in a rug every night.

Parents say "sorry" to folks who've just met you.

They make it all better when something's upset you.

And once they have fixed all your problems . . .

and pickles,

you'd better watch out because parents love . . .

...TICKLES!